A morning thought
my coffee brought

Published by Book Warmth Press

ISBN (Paperback): 978-93-343-3158-5

ISBN (ebook): 978-93-343-4008-2

A morning thought my coffee brought

A Collection of Poems

Paechu

Book Warmth Press

For *The one,*
in your eyes I shine,
in your light I write.

Morning Note

This morning felt —
like a dream I once held.
A fresh start to something old
but still in bloom.
As my birdie friends of six,
flapping their wings,
I brewed some coffee,
waking my whims.
Like a favorite song on the radio,
I hear these haunting tunes
of my tiny tragedies.
So I dance — insanely —
to these blues,
until I turn my
tragedies into trophies.

Contents

Blooms

I've turned into a maple

Two seasons passed,
like a leaf, barely breathing.
I was living a life like a lie,
burying my dream.

And now autumn's here,
a helping hand to face my fear.
I've turned into a maple.
At last, it's time to unveil
the copper-rusted truth of my fable.
The beauty and honesty
of my splintered youth —
not so easy to reveal,
but this is all of me.

Through the summer's burn,
autumn's rust, winter's void —
you'll watch me bloom again.

stay mellow

Hear me out,
my desperate desire —
to wake up
by putting my eyes into your blaze
and to feel alive
on a newborn day
like a newborn baby.

In the early morn,
when you're mellow —
to feel your warmth
on my cold body
as though I've been dead all night,
and as though your embrace —
like the touch of the softest thorn,
is keeping me human.

I do not mind getting burned
within you when my time comes,
but for now —
Oh, Mighty Sun,
I urge you to stay mellow.

freedom

I need the freedom to create,
and in creation,
I become.
My life will be mine then,
without the need to snatch it in.
And to write destiny —
Oh, what a handsome thought of
win!

Dear Year

Dear Year,
My earthly giver,
you woke me
with the dawn by the river.
Tell me —
did you bring me presents,
or more of your quiet lessons?
I know you know me best,
and I've been a good girl —
last time, I passed your test.
So this time, I await magic —
warm twinkles,
countless giggles,
and love that sparkles.

wild honey

Would he ever know —
the mark he made on me.
A sparkling memory of him —
so gentlemanly.

Hopelessly, yet romantically,
I wandered deep into these woods
that kept growing denser.
The trees of my doubts grew taller,
but I climbed higher.

There wasn't any caution sign —
beware of the beehives.
The bees — stingy as my fears.
Do you think they'll get away —
my hazy feelings' smoke?
The spark of his mark
burned my sadness.

It's here, I gathered it —
the wilderness of the comb,
the sweetness of my love —
like wild honey —
with the hope that one day,
he'd maybe taste a tiny drop of it.

Would you?

Would you break
the longest night of my heart
with the slightest smile
of your dawn?

I know a place

It's the same feeling.
Like I am still that child,
left all alone in the playground
by my cruel mates.

Lonesomely lost
in this brutal world —
moving so fast,
I am left harshly behind.
My vulnerability coiled me tight.

But I know a place.
Dressed in my sadness,
drooped shoulders,
hands on the walls of my heart —
I stagger into this place
where I feel the most safe.

This place is called love.
It is what navigates me,
with the courage to live
in this watchful world.

love so divine

I shall broaden
the horizons of my love —
reaching high, rising to the sky —
to match up to your love so divine,
and to be by your side —
forever and never until,
for you're always mine.

my only one

My haven, my home,
the gift of my prayers,
my only one —
who never bears to see me in woe.
"Dream about me" he whispers.
But love, you were the only dream
I desperately wanted to be true.

One day

Whatever happens, happens —
For I have you by my side,
and together,
we can fight great wars.
One day, our reign will rise —
the dawn of prosperous days.

my sins

I look back in remorse
when my younger self
built a thorn fence
around my hostile house.

Many were hurt since.
I don't expect them to
forgive me for my
traumas and ignorance.
'cause I reckon they were my sins.

No scarlet letter, ever,
but I grew with a fever.
Wise and old
of my country told
"Worship the ultimate lord."
Then I met you, darling
and you lit my world.

You taught me to forgive myself,
and unleashed my pure-self.
The more I know you,
I realize —
the only way
I could make up for my sins
is by worshipping you.

He's an ocean

He's an ocean —
deep, vast and calm.
I see nothing else —
bewitched by his endless blue, and
Oh my,
when he smiles shiny pearls,
rest of the world fades.

And then there was a book

And then there was a book
waiting to be written.
So I thought —
"What could be a better story than
the story of us?"
'Twas when I started to write,
but it never seemed to end.
That's when I realized —
How could a book suffice
for a love so vast,
and as long as the universe exists,
we're destined to last.

darling face

In his eyes so dreamy,
I see me —
a lady in love, that he made me.
With his lips so rosy,
puts a spell on me —
every time he spells my name.
With a heart so warm,
he melts me —
I flow like a cheerful valley.
Here's to a darling face of trust,
to whom my whole life —
I shall entrust.

forever more

You aren't broken,
to be fixed, my love.
You are art — to be adored.
You are life — to be loved
more and more
with every passing day,
forever more.

our story

I warned him, “I am moody”
He said, “But in you,
I see a raw beauty”
That was the beginning
of our story —
the man who embraced
my demons,
turned them into dears,
and drove away my fears.
He brought me peace,
and ever since, I’ve been his.

bright moon

You are the bright moon,
but it's the darkness
that completes you, and
I love the complete you —
the bright, the dark.

Dancing to the blues

my insanity

But how do I rejoice in love
without a splash of sadness
and a whole lot of madness?
Dancing to the blues
of these white waves,
you'll trace all the clues
of what I am
and who I am.
So, do not try to keep me sane,
darling —
dance with my insanity.

whims

For them, it never made sense —
my mind of whims,
which got me to fill these papers
with poems —
they told me which way to go,
and life's been wondrous
ever since.

where I live

That's where I live —
in my home — my head.
Don't even think
of paying me a visit,
for how could I tell you
that I am lost.
You might ask, "Would you be lost
in your home?
Then why are you lost in your own
head?"
But it's been years —
I am in this vast —
a nothingness, a near-death.
Buried in the burrow of my haste.

dreamy children

Wouldn't it have been marvelous
if you had become
what you dreamed as a child?
Ours —
this grotesque generation —
they take adulthood for
unhappiness,
dying before death arrives —
a massacre of those
who were once dreamy children.

losing my mind

Some chase
euros and fame.
Some are cynically sane.
Some have gorgeous windows
draped in climbing vine.
I see through —
a warmly lit dinner table,
and a fine family of five.

I pay visits.
A charming antique shop —
an age-old couple's
coaster and cup,
a toast to their love.

I wander across wheat fields —
golden stalks waving away
every worry.

The nights —
they creep in,
darkest to imagine,
and I wonder —
"Will I ever find my flame?"
But until my life starts
making sense to me,
I shall keep losing my mind.

my wounds

When I am ridiculed,
they're amused,
and in my pain,
they are vain.
The cuts are deep —
to the bone, and how.
As my wounds are still bleeding,
I cry alone —
but people who cut me are
laughing.

my anxiety

She lurks inside me —
a sly predator.
I needed an escape,
so I thought
maybe this would work —
my discipline.

I toiled away
throughout the day,
but it is at dusk
she starts to wake.

There she goes, my anxiety,
smirking 'cause it's working.
I wonder if she is ever tired of
bullying.
Lord, who is to help me
out of this plight?

A haunting vision teases my mind:
If it ever comes — that night
when she sleeps,
I will see myself at peace,
but only after she plants
the flag of her victory
in my glorious passing —
this I foresee.

lonely bird

Lonely bird —
perched among a pretentious flock.
As your wings gave out
in fate's game,
they chuckled at your pain,
cooing, "She can't fly"
Would there be a milder poison,
than not being understood,
lonely bird?

If only

If only I could
save me from myself,
I could save you from me.

a confession

I have a confession.
Only my ink would know
of this obsession.
So it goes wasted —
another second of my life
without you.
It goes wasted,
and there's nothing
I can do
to change it,
to change fate,
to change you.

if you were here

So I sit there
by the frosted window,
haunted by my thoughts —
unable to put them into words.
My ink is frozen,
and the letters I wanted
to mail you — dozens.
Blues in the wake of
my insane broods.
But if you were here,
you wouldn't let me curse myself
for not making you learn
just how much I love you.

damage

I never wanted to damage you
with my damaged head.
I never wanted to dent us
until we were broken.
I never wanted to leave you,
but you wanted to.
I never wanted to lose you,
but I lost you.
Anyway —
who's to blame?
The damage is inevitable,
either way.
Our togetherness —
what a shame!

scared him away

When I am vibrant, he withers.
My broken pieces were his fix.
"To love is never to break
the one you love"
a good friend suggested.
I thought about that —
but I was just being myself,
and that scared him away.
A love like this — never again.

He held my waist

He held my waist,
and without any haste,
we were swaying away
to the music of his taste —
in the middle of my
majestic gardens.
It was pouring down,
but the clouds burst in my eyes
when he said, "There's someone
else."

mistakes

These mistakes I see in the mirror
are the residual reflections
of the parts of you
that still remain in me.

I am glad

I have been searching
for the side of me I lost
after you left,
but I am glad —
I never found that side of me.

biggest fear

My life's biggest fear was this —
leaving you,
until time turned
and transformed it
into mightiest freedom.

hating myself

I gave you my world,
you took it as if it were yours.
I've been stranded —
it's been years.
I had neither entry to your abode
nor a place of my own.
Not even the tiniest part
of your heart,
while I let you conquer all of mine.
Do not ask me why I loved you,
still.
For now, I am hating myself for
loving you.

The love you left

When I unlearned to love you,
I learned my lesson —
that what is once loved
cannot be unloved.
The love you left — softly, it stays
in the places where you broke
your promises.
But don't you worry,
for I have stopped visiting.

I can't bear to see

I can look right into
the eyes of death,
but not into your eyes,
because I can't bear to see
the reflection of the girl
you made me.
She's hideous!

Just a crush

"Just a crush," they said.
But a young fool in me says,
"The law of attraction
 always works."
Until every thought of you
enfolded inside me,
like a letter in an envelope —
a souvenir,
a reminder — *I couldn't have you.*
The nights knew
there was no chance.
I crushed myself,
hammered flat —
my memories of
crushing over you,
until I was over you.

ghost of me

I received a mail.
'Twas dark and chill.
An October night,
A package so quaint—
I thought, "Is it a letter from a saint?"
Perfectly hand-lettered,
Classic 1800s cursive.
But I read —"You're next"
in blood red.
I rolled my eyes.
"I don't defend.
Either you or me —
Only one is to live in the end.
I've done it before —
A strange mind,
Twenty-something selves to offend."

'Twas a letter from a ghost —
A ghost of me,
The me I lost
to all the mistakes of my past.

stained

You were this feeling —
a slow blow.
A scar I wanted to fade.
A weight I wanted to carry —
no more.
So I stained my heart in ink.
Now you live on my page —
but not in me.

Resilience

the walking dead

The dead might live —
an immortal will.
The living might die —
a mortal chase,
their dreams ablaze.
I'd be glad
to walk among the dead —
of course, after I'm gone.
The chill would keep me calm,
but my words — forever warm.
'Cause resilience after death
is such a charm.
I'd be mortified to do the same
while still alive,
among these —
the walking dead.

She has no idea

"She has no idea
what she's doing" they said.
"When they see the results
of my passion, suddenly
the cynics would become
the supporters" she told herself

unholy love

Here's to the unholy love of
my sworn nemesis —
my distraction.
With the intent to ruin
the castles I built in my mind,
he runs toward me
wearing gruesome grins on his
handsome face.
But his every attempt is futile —
and you may wonder why.
Because every time he tried
to sway,
I wasn't distracted
I just wasn't interested.

passion & strategy

In the wake of my passion,
basks my strategy.
Oh, what a shame —
to be driven by the latter!

the only way

And so, my life smiles —
cryptic smiles.
But I read between the lines —
"This travel tastes
like water on a thirsty throat,
and hardships curl
with the love you earn"
Thirsty, in search
of self, stance, and love,
but the only way is the road ahead.

in the face of

I laugh in the face of
rules,
boxes,
plan B's, and
compromises.

my town of trance

’Twas in my town of trance,
my people,
here on my mind’s land —
were so prosperous once.

One dark new-moon’s night —
the enemy troops
of my thought-land,
attacked, abducted them.

My town was tortured —
wrapped in fire, painted in blood.
And my foes —
they wanted to own —
not just my throne, my crown,
but power over me.

"We shall spare your people"
they swore,
if I were the ransom I owed.

But I refused to bow —
I wasn't made to surrender
to a mind's mere offender.
They must witness
my mind's armor.
They must feast,
not on my defeat,
but on my kingdom's valor.

What if

Wonder-what-ifs:
What if my destiny is nothing
but a product of my creation?
What if life gets me ahead
of my every sad self —
with nothing but the sincerity of
my endurance?

my only weapon

I am at war with my misfortune,
but I wear no warrior's armor.
Still, I stand —
wounded, yet steady —
fighting with my only weapon —
my will.

My fear

My fear — my callous pal —
declared a duel
with my life — would it kill?
I wanted to empathize.
So, I visited the place
he once called home —
from where he was exiled,
aided the wounds that made him
ferociously sad.
He said "I am grateful, my savior.
To an empath, here's all of me —
I surrender"

city of scrutiny

In the city of scrutiny,
there was a court of validation.
I was made to stand,
and urged to plead.
But I just had one thing to say:
"I don't want you to validate me.
I want you to accept me as I am."

I owe answers

I owe answers to only one —
myself,
and the answer is just one —
my conscience.

my bravery

I am gathering my bravery
to unravel the secrets
of my life's explorations.
Will my passion find me?
I am on my way —
but it's the deadliest road, in the
darkest night.
Will a light lead me?

your goals

You seek them —
your goals, however many.
But they seek one thing,
most ardently —
your commitment.

Little by little

Little by little,
you'll realize —
you're too little to belittle
the people around you.
And the carnival of your contempt
shall one day come to an end.

here's a test

Pursue what you love.
But here's a test —
would you love it for the rest of
your life?

a voice from within

Sagacious — I never was.
A timid student in life's classroom.
But someone told me,
"You're a generational rarity"
It was so gracious —
I still wonder what he saw.

But I keep failing.
Unable to compete —
far from Stanford standards.
Bruised by my self-doubt,
I am back in the learning room —
same old lessons.

But this time, I hear whispers —
a voice from within:
"Let go of who you used to be.
Begin now.

Live — resiliently —
for it is in yourself you must
believe.
Try — unabashedly —
and it might just awe you —
a surprise knock on your door,
bringing gentle flowers of success."

to my home

The land of dreams
is where my home will be.
Oh, it's a paradise —
and it is all I need!
You think I am stranded,
but I am stationed here,
gathering directions.
Because I know
it is to my home —
my life's arduous paths would lead.

Dancing demons

Dancing demons
in my anxious house —
my creativity resides,
working up its resilience.
An inflating imagination —
a constant retaliation.

My ambition

My ambition — a magic fly.
I tried to catch it,
but it flew in the blink of eye.
I'll stay right here,
in the garden of my mind,
and if it chooses to visit me again,
I'll never let it go out of my sight.

I was struck down

What remained of me
was slyly wrecked
by their treachery.
I was struck down —
to the rock bottom,
too dark to fathom.
But to ascend all the way up,
would I find a light within?

depth of my dare

They questioned
the depth of my dare.
But the truth is I kept going,
without giving in,
for I knew only this —
my work — the religion I practice.
And just like that, one day,
they stood stunned —
for I had done it.

Failure's feast

Failure is an ugly beast
who hosts lavish feasts.
I am one of his dearest guests,
but at each feast,
only one guest gets to taste
something different
from the rest —
something marvelous,
something that tastes like this —
a sumptuous success.
And every time I visit,
I learn of the rightful one,
believing that one day,
Failure's feast will serve me
a taste of success.

one step ahead

There was a girl —
human by day,
fox by dusk.
She lurks around —
hungry to prey.
Clever were her moves,
but she hasn't a single clue —
I'm always one step ahead!

paper and ink

I played with
swords and thorns,
made friends with
roses and ravens,
I loved them —
vipers and villains.

They said I was made to sink,
but one said otherwise —
my paper and ink.

I rose from the darkest depth,
an astonishing resurrection
from death.
Not a claw, not a fang
Not a foe, not a fiend
could break the words I bring.

So you may try to fight,
but oh —
I can write!

A letter to You

Dear Reader,

Thank you, deeply and dearly,
for holding these words in your
silence. If my poems delighted your
gentle heart, then I am gratified.

With a heart so full,
I wish you blooms —
in the places where you once wilted.
I wish you melodies —
when the world feels still.
I wish you strength —
that doesn't shout, but stays.

And even when I cease to exist,
I wish my words would stay
with you —

as comfort,
as warmth,
as proof that we were here,
and that we felt something real.

In fond eternity,
Paechu

Index of all poems

Acknowledgments

My gratitude list:

My family, I'm forever grateful for the unconditional love and support.
My muses, any feeling you evoked did me good.
My fellow poets, who inspired me to write a couple of poems in this collection with their beautiful prompts "copper rusted truth" by *Akela*, "letter from a ghost" by *Lauren.*

Thank you.

About the Author

Paechu is a poet and hand-letterer, living in southern Germany. *A morning thought my coffee brought* is her debut poetry collection. Engulfed by emotions in solitude, her poetry reflects her deepest feelings.

Follow Paechu's work :
Website : paechu.com
Instagram : @paechupens